Puppy Mudge
Finds a Friend

Puppy Mudge Finds a Friend

By Cynthia Rylant

Illustrated by Suçie Stevenson

SCHOLASTIC INC.
New York Toronto London Auckland Sydney
Mexico City New Delhi Hong Kong Buenos Aires

ISBN 0-439-77325-3
Text copyright © 2004 by Cynthia Rylant.
Illustrations copyright © 2004 by Suçie Stevenson. All rights reserved.
Published by Scholastic Inc., 557 Broadway, New York, NY 10012,
by arrangement with Simon & Schuster Books for Young Readers,
Simon & Schuster Children's Publishing Division.
SCHOLASTIC and associated logos are
trademarks and/or registered trademarks of Scholastic Inc.

12 11 10 9 8 7 6 5 4 3 2   5 6 7 8 9 10/0

Printed in the U.S.A.   23

First Scholastic printing, September 2005
Book design by Lucy Ruth Cummins
The text for this book is set in Goudy.
The illustrations for this book are rendered in pen-and-ink and watercolor.

This is Puppy Mudge.
He lives with Henry.

Mudge likes it.

He likes a lot of things.

He likes chew toys.

He likes crackers.

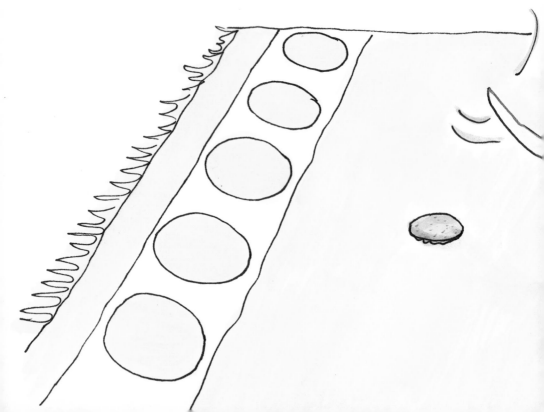

He likes to drool.

(Mudge drools a lot.)

Mudge also likes cats.

Mudge found a cat friend.

Her name is Fluffy.

Mudge and Fluffy play.

Fluffy runs.

Mudge runs.

Fluffy hides.

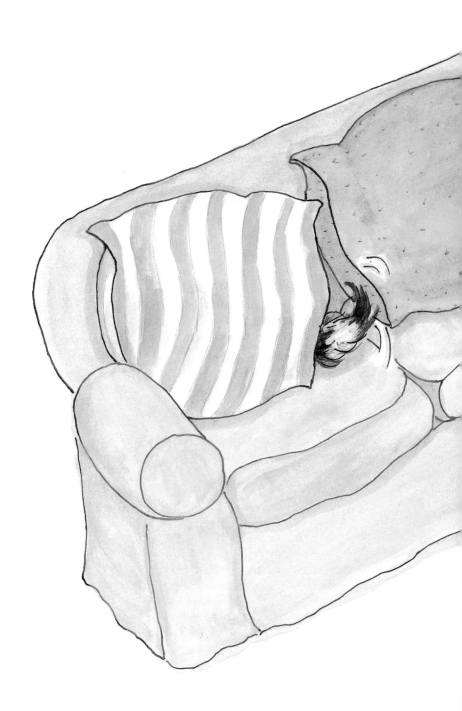

Mudge hides.

Fluffy climbs.

Mudge does not.

Fluffy and Mudge play and play.

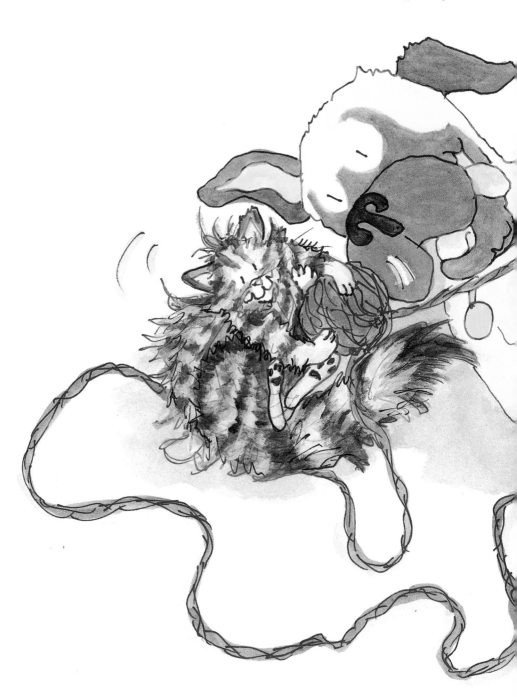

Then they rest.

Fluffy purrs.
Mudge snores.

Friends.